WINTER WONDER DADDY

JOE SATORIA

This book is sold subject to the condition that it shall not, by way of trade or otherwise, be lent, re-sold, duplicated, hired out, or otherwise circulated without the publisher's prior written consent in any form of binding or cover other than that in which it is published and without similar condition including this condition being imposed on the subsequent purchaser.

WINTER WONDER DADDY
JOE SATORIA

Copyright © 2022 Joe Satoria
All Rights Reserved

ISBN: 9798366349246

Satoria Publishing © 2022

This is a work of fiction. All characters and events portrayed in this novel are fictitious and are products of the author's imagination and any resemblance to actual events, or locales or persons, living or dead are entirely coincidental.

www.JoeSatoria.com

Content: Daddy/little, low angst, holiday, dual POV.

MORE *MY LITTLE'S WISHLIST*:
Cookie Cutter Daddy
Winter Wonder Daddy
Sugar Sweet Daddy

Contents

ONE	1
TWO	11
THREE	20
FOUR	30
FIVE	39
SIX	50
SEVEN	58
EIGHT	66
NINE	77
TEN	88
EPILOGUE	98
AUTHOR'S NOTE	103
About the Author	104

ONE

KAMDEN

Green wasn't my color, and work wasn't my thing. And being made to dress in an itchy elf costume felt like punishment. I suppose it was almost punishment. I was working to make extra cash to buy a life-size teddy bear.

Recently, my dad told me that money didn't grow on trees. Shock. My family were financially supportive of me and my art. And since I hadn't sold any pieces in a while, I didn't have the funds for my big cuddly teddy bear boyfriend. To realize my Christmas wish, I was helping at the town mall. My dad was the manager, so it was nepotism, except without any of the glamor.

In the changing area, a room off the break room, I

looked at myself in the hideous shade of green. I was an elf. Usually, I loved dressing up and role play. But the itch this outfit gave me wasn't good.

I had to be out on the mall floor working in Santa's grotto, handing out gifts to children. I didn't mind, it was easy. The last time I needed extra cash, all I had to do to was to work as an office assistant here.

"Kam," my dad's voice called to me, standing in the doorway of the changing room. "There's a Santa out there without an elf."

My eyes rolled back. "Dad, do I—"

He snapped a picture, chuckling to himself.

"Fine, I'm going."

Snapping more pictures of me, blinding me with the flash in my face. "Your mom wanted a picture," he said. "You know, just a couple days of this. Maybe a week, how much did you ask for?"

I cocked a hand on my hip. "Take another picture of me like this, and I'll tell mom you're bullying me."

"You're twenty-six, Kam," he said. "Your mom asked me to bully you. She wants to know when we're getting a new painting."

"Soon, like after Christmas." I shrugged. "But it won't happen at all if you humiliate me."

"Character building," he said. "And I'm gonna make sure you stay out there all day."

I had two Christmas wishes. The first was to have a giant

teddy to cuddle at night. A second wish, if I were lucky enough, would be to have a hot, Daddy of a man. I wanted to be in the middle of a cuddle sandwich. One giant teddy, me, and a hot Daddy.

Out on the mall floor, I saw a man dressed in an ill-fitting Santa suit. He didn't look like the Santa who'd been working earlier in the week. That man had been old with a naturally gray beard. This man wore one of those white beards with the elastic that went around his head and ears.

Walking by all the screaming children and their parents. My job was letting them in, giving them an *I've Seen Santa* sticker, then giving them a gift bag. Each bag had bubbles, a plastic animal, some coloring pages, and crayons or pens, depending on how old they were.

"Hi Santa," I said, approaching the man on the grand faux gold chair. "I haven't seen you around. Where did they drag you in from?"

"Mascots," he said. "Usually walking around in the penguin costume."

"Ok, slay," I said, snapping my finger. "Gimme your best Santa impression."

He chuckled. "Ho, ho, ho." His voice going deeper.

"Your look too young to be Santa. Is it your first time?" I asked.

"First time for everything," he said, winking at me.

"I—" I was caught off-guard by the wink. "I'll get to work."

I didn't know what he looked like behind that red suit or hat, and the thick fake beard. I wanted to know what he looked like, I wanted to know how to interpret the wink. Although I was probably easy if he asked. I tried to see who he was behind the beard and the hat and the heavy suit. There was something about him that seemed familiar, like someone I'd probably seen a lot of before. Here I was, standing, smiling, and being a damn good elf with my face on show for the entire world, and he got to sit and hide behind all that beard. His deep brown eyes, every time they connected with my gaze felt like someone was tickling their finger into my ribcage.

After what felt like hours of work, we were given a break. All the way back to the break room of the mall, I walked back with him.

"I'm Gage, by the way," he finally said.

We were away from everyone, except the people coming in and out of the break room.

I continued to stare into his eyes, wondering if there was anything else to take from him. I needed to know more. I needed to know who he was.

Standing by the coffee pot, he chuckled, breaking eye contact to dig around in a cupboard for a mug. "So, what do I call you?"

"Yeah, you can call me," I said. "I mean. It's Kamden, or Kam, or—"

"You mind pouring the coffee?" he asked, tugging at the

beard on his face. "I need to get this off, it's starting to itch."

"Itch." My mind, seemingly only catching the last words of anything he said. "This itches too." Although it hadn't itched in a while.

"The coffee," he said.

"Right, right. Coffee, coffee, coffee. I love coffee." It came out of nowhere. Immediate embarrassment like a blazing heat whacked me. "I—oh my god."

Gage at least laughed. I was preoccupied trying to see him remove the beard and hat like he'd been wearing a disguise.

Salt and pepper hair, like a dark slate, all slicked back from where he'd been wearing the Santa hat. He had a trimmed beard and extremely cut cheekbones. Absorbed in his looks, I almost poured hot coffee all over the countertop.

"This thing is worse than the mascot costume," he said, ruffling his fingers through his hair. "I'd take the suit off, but I'm actually wearing another layer with stuffing inside." He puffed out his cheeks and sighed.

Handing him a coffee, we sat together at a table. There was a sofa, where one woman sat staring at the TV screen as it played the in-mall advertising.

"So, I probably have seen you around then."

"As the mascot, yeah," he chuckled. "Out of it, I'm not too sure."

"You prefer the mascot to the Santa gig then?"

He hummed, sipping his coffee. "I'm only stepping in for Santa. But I don't find it half bad. I mean, I get to sit on that comfy ass chair all day." His voice was a little different compared to the voice he'd been using as Santa. It wasn't as hoarse. "What about you?"

That was a tough one. I didn't want to outright say why I was doing this, because it could sound bad. "I'm just trying to save a little extra cash."

"Cool, I'm also a freelance photographer as well," he said. "Although it doesn't really pay the bills for me right now, but I'm sure, one day, I'll have my own coffee table book filled with photos I've taken."

Seeing his eyes light up with passion as he spoke about it made me want to curl up into a ball and lay on his lap. "I love that," I mumbled under my breath. "You know, I'm a painter. I—" I was giving away too much about myself. I had to hold back, I couldn't reveal everything, he'd probably think I was crazy.

"Artists always find each other," he chuckled. "What type of stuff do you paint?"

I couldn't tell him it was art I made when I was in my little space. "Just things I find interesting. You know, people, mostly."

He smacked a hand at the soft padding on his chest. "What about me?" He smirked, so much confidence in one simple facial expression. "You think you'd paint me?"

"It all depends." I took the coffee cup to my mouth to

keep myself from saying anymore.

Break was almost over. It was short, but it gave me enough mental energy to get through the rest of the day.

There was something about Gage. He was warm and engaging. Plus, he was a fellow arty person. He was right about that. We did flock together. If only there was some way I could give him a sign, maybe a wink back, but knowing my luck, I'd wink with both eyes; everyone knew that was called a blink.

He'd raced on ahead of me to the changing room once we'd finished. Which was fine, since I'd seen my dad approaching and I didn't want Gage to see the two of us talking.

"How was it?" he asked, grinning at me. "Your mom messaged you; did you get it?"

"No, you told me I wasn't allowed my phone out here with me."

"Surprised you actually listened," he said. "But how was it, standing on your feet all day knowing you were working to get paid?"

"It was one way to kill time." I played it off as if I didn't enjoy any of it. Obviously, a lie. I enjoyed being near Gage. He'd crack funny jokes to the kids when they sat on his lap, and they'd leave with the goodie bag from me and laughter from him. They also definitely believed he was Santa, and that was magical to see. It spoke to the little in me, believing in Santa was wholesome and it tickled me deep inside.

"Tomorrow, same again," he said. "And try to visit your mom at the community center. You know it's only across the road from your apartment."

"Dad," I threw my head back and groaned. "Every time I go over there, she always ropes me into something."

"You know a lot of it runs on volunteer work," he said.

I stared at him, my eyes in squints and my brows pinched together. "Fine, I'll go over, but you know I need inspiration. I need to paint and draw."

He clicked his tongue. "And we haven't seen any of your new stuff," he said. "What happened to that gallery you were talking to?"

The truth was, I didn't feel comfortable showing off the art I was making right now. It was a lot of scribble art. It was how a lot of my high school textbooks looked like at the end of the year. The pages covered in scribbles of all different things. Except, as an adult, and an artist, that meant scribbles but on a grander scale.

"We can talk about this later," I said. "I wanna get changed."

"Fine. And of course, it goes without saying, I support you and your art. I love you, and if you don't feel ready to show us what you're working on, I respect that," he said.

I nodded to him, keeping a straight face. "Did mom make you rehearse that?"

He snickered. "Yes, but only because I have a very talented son and you know we have that space on the wall.

I want another one of your paintings up there."

On my current strike of inspiration, he wasn't going to be receiving any of the paintings I'd been working on. "I'll think about it." There was nothing to think about.

Dad left as I went to the changing room.

Gage was the only one in there, hat and beard off. He sat, scrolling through his phone. Perking up as I came in. "Hey."

"Hi," I said, letting out a yawn from nowhere. "Oh wow. Today has drained me."

Smiling, he nodded. "Same. I can't even begin to take this suit off. It's like a second layer of skin now."

Looking him up and down. He looked like a poorly padded drag queen. "How much padding is in there?"

"Too much," he said, smacking his knee. "I don't even feel that."

"Wow."

"You want to sit and see if I can feel you?"

Knowing nobody was in the changing room with us, I still looked around. "No, I—"

"Come on," he said, smacking at his knee again. "It'll be fun."

Maybe both our ideas of fun did have a cross-section.

I sat on his knee, perching, trying not to apply weight.

"What do you want for Christmas?" he asked in his deep Santa voice. "Ho, ho, ho."

"I can't tell you," I said. "Since I know you're not the

real Santa."

"I might not be Santa, but I've been known to please," he chuckled.

I giggled. "Naughty Santa. Wait—Santa?" I asked, feigning a gasp. "Is that a candy cane in your pants, or are you—"

"Oh, this—that's actually a candy cane," he said, pulling out the red and white striped candy cane. He presented it to me.

I accepted it. It would've been rude not to. "And the vibration—what the—" It tickled on my thigh.

"Crap, I think that's my phone," he said.

As he took his call, I sucked on the candy cane and slowly changed. I was nosey and listened to part of his call. He seemed pissed. But I couldn't stop listening. And as I turned to see him, I saw a tattoo on his forearm. It was a line art hand holding a rainbow flag. That came as a surprise.

Santa was gay.

TWO

GAGE

Of everything going on in my day, the last thing I expected to happen would be my roommate, Alexia calling me to tell me that our apartment building was being fumigated. She'd told me why, some bug, or something. My brain was in overdrive, trying the hardest to think about what I was going to do.

It was the middle of winter and right before Christmas. I wasn't going to get a hotel room anywhere. Alexia was lucky, she had her boyfriend's place to stay until the fumigation was over, and apparently that could take a week. An entire week would take us right up to Christmas Eve.

"Are you listening?" her voice chimed in my ear. "I tried

to call you earlier so you could come get clothes. They've taped the entire building up."

Undressing from my Santa suit and the padded body suit beneath it, I only had the clothes I came into work with today. "I—"

"Gage, I can ask Sam if you can stay on the sofa, but he lives with two other guys."

"Right. It's fine," I said. "I'll think of something."

"If you need anything, I'll do what I can to help you," she said.

I sighed, turning and glancing at Kamden as he was slowly changing from his elf costume. He was clearly listening, and I didn't care. "Is anything going to be damaged?"

"No, they're just going through all the apartments," she said. "So, I guess they'll find those sex toys in your closet."

Choking, I knew Kamden couldn't hear, but part of me thought he could. "If they find mine, they'll find yours." It wasn't an extensive collection of toys, just a couple.

Hanging up, I rolled my head back and stared at the fluorescent ceiling lights of the changing room.

"Everything ok?" Kamden asked.

After the playful flirting with him, I didn't want to ruin it now by telling him I was effectively homeless for the week.

"So, you wanna go get a drink or something?" he continued. "There's this bar and they make some really good Christmas cocktails." He slipped a sweater over his head. He looked so incredibly cuddly.

"I can't," I said.

"I get it. I get it. You're handsome. You've probably got a boyfriend and all that."

The flirting bore fruit. "No, I don't. I'm just homeless."

"Homeless?" his expression changed. "I'm sorry. You know, my mom runs a community center in the town if you need assistance with housing."

And he was nice. Usually, people would run a mile, especially if they told me they were homeless. "Technically, my apartment is being fumigated. Someone called pest control, or whatever, and they've forced an entire apartment block out for fumigation." I rubbed my thumb and finger in my eyes. The chill in the air now since the padding of the body suit was off. I sat in my boxer briefs and a tight white vest.

"Oh, well I'm sure there's a hotel open somewhere," he said.

"My roommate already checked. Not a one. It's fine. I'll probably just sleep in my car or something. I'm sure I can grab a sleeping bag from a store here."

His expression changed once more, maybe relief. "Obviously, you can't do that. So, why don't you stay the night at mine?"

"No, I can't. I just met you." And I wanted to sleep with him, which I knew was just a feeling that would pass. I got like that when I was in proximity with cute guys.

"I literally have a huge ass apartment, if you don't stay on my sofa, then I'll just feel awful," he said, cocking his hip to the side. "And then my mom would make it into this huge thing because I didn't make sure you were fine."

He was adorable and getting stressed. "Your mom?" I asked.

"Yeah, I told you, she runs the community center, they help loads of people. I'll obviously have to mention you to her, and maybe score brownie points."

"Brownie points?" I stood, stretching my chest. Kamden stared, probably because my nipples were hard in the vest. The changing room was cold. He was lucky he didn't get a peek at something else.

"Yeah. You know, so—" he paused, his eyes were going wild, up and down on my body. "So, I'm offering you my sofa for the night. And—and I suppose until your apartment is ready for you to go back."

Clicking my tongue, I looked him back up and down. "Well, if you ask me, I think we're moving too fast. We just met, now you're inviting me over."

"Then I guess we need to get to know each other a little better," he said. "And you should probably get dressed before we do that."

It was a good idea, and that was one way to get to know each other. I also liked the other way of getting to know each other, and that involved two naked bodies coming together, and quite literally cumming together. "I'm not really in a position to refuse," I said.

Kamden turned away, scoffing into a giggle. "I'm not forcing you; I'm just being nice."

"You know, I'll take you up on the offer. But you'll have to let me pay for drinks," I said.

"Great. I can let you do that," he snickered. "There's a restaurant and bar near my apartment. So, maybe we could grab something to eat as well. Since, I've been on my feet all day handing out gift bags."

"I'll pay for dinner as well," I said. "Just let me get dressed. You also have some place I can wash my clothes at yours?"

"I have a machine, it's a washer-drier."

That was enough of what I needed to know, at least I could have my clothes cleaned. I wore a cream t-shirt with a faded graphic design on it, a pair of gray ripped jeans, boots with snow grips on them, and a thick blue coat with fur on the hood. I could've probably slept in the coat; it was warm enough.

We drove separately into the town. I followed him. I was from the outskirts of the town. I went to Hinton High School, but I never really came to the town. It was an extra thirty minutes to drive into the closest city than it was to drive into town. The town was covered in a layer of snow, untouched, no sight of footprints, even though I could see people walking in it.

Parking beside Kamden, I wondered what I was doing. I'd accepted his help, and we'd been flirting all day, but that's probably where it had to end. I had a type, and I didn't know if he fit in with that type.

He knocked on my window. "Come on," he said. "The restaurant is up here." His voice muffled.

I looked back in my car, seeing my backpack from my work locker on the backseat. I knew the crime rate in town was low, but right now, I couldn't afford to lose anything else. I'd already lost a comfy bed for the week.

On Main Street, there was a small restaurant, *Sorvino's*. The name seemed Italian. Inside, there were people at tables and sitting at booths. Gentle Christmas music played, and the entire place was decoration like it had ransacked one of the holiday stores at the mall.

We were led to a booth and handed menus.

Before the server could leave, Kamden placed his drink order. "Cocktails, I want the Grinch one."

"Oh, delicious," the server said. "And for you, sir?"

"I'll—" I locked eyes with Kamden across the table. "What's a Grinch?"

"The Grinch is that guy who stole Christmas in the film," Kamden said, a big grin on his face. "But they do this amazing citrus and cherry drink, and it's green."

"Ok, what's the alcohol?" I asked.

"Rum."

"I'll take one of those as well. I trust your judgement," I

said, locking eyes with Kamden.

"Ok, I'll get those ready for you, then I'll be back to take your food order," she said, smiling at us. As she walked off, she swished away with that pep I only saw appear around Christmastime.

We sat in quiet for a moment as Kamden scrolled on his phone and I looked through my backpack in the seat beside me. I had my camera equipment and laptop in there, but not a change of clothes. Which was appropriate for me, more concerned with what I had rather than what I could wear. If I thought about it, I'd probably consider myself a nudist.

"You probably shouldn't trust my judgement," he said. "I have really bad judgement, just FYI."

"How else does someone end up working at a Santa's grotto?" I snickered.

"I'd say ending up working with you was worth it."

The server brought us our almost neon green drinks. They even had a cocktail stick with a cherry on top, almost like it wore a Christmas hat.

"I'll take a pasta carbonara," he said. "And maybe a plate of fries." He locked eyes with me. "To share."

"And—" I'd barely looked over the menu. "I'll take the—" I placed a finger on the menu, going down and stopping. "Ravioli, with the ricotta and spinach."

"Good choice," the server said, scribbling them down and walking off.

Kamden lifted his cocktail glass. "Cheers," he said.

"Cheers."

"Now, let's get to know each other. So, when did you lose your virginity?"

With my lip to the glass, I almost sputtered at how forward his question was. "Jeez."

"I saw the tattoo, is that—"

Rolling my arm over on the table to show off the tattoo, I nodded. "Yes, I'm gay."

"You know I'm gay, right?"

He wasn't exactly subtle in his mannerisms. "Breaking news," I said, trying to keep a straight face. "When did you come out?"

"I've always been out," he said. "Hard to keep me in, I think. What about you?"

"I came out in college," I told him. "I was probably like nineteen, just turned twenty, maybe. I kinda always knew."

"What did you go to college for?"

"Dropped out, actually," I said. "But I went to an arts college for a little while. I get bored easy, and it mostly felt like I was paying to network sometimes."

He smiled and nodded. "I went to an arts college too."

"Then you know how I feel. You pay the tuition, and it just feels like you're paying so much just to network with guests and have your work in a gallery, a gallery you basically paid for a spot in with tuition." I could've gone on a small tirade. I paused myself, trying not to seem like I was some jaded ass. But there was a gallery in Hinton I'd been in contact with about showcasing some of my photography.

"I feel the same," he said. "Except, I didn't drop out."

"You're a little sassy, do you get sassier when you've had a drink?" I asked, hoping he would.

"Wait and see," he said, sucking back the cocktail.

I was crushing hard on him. Maybe because he was giving me a sofa to sleep on tonight, or maybe because he had a little bite to whatever he was saying. I liked it, but I didn't know if we shared the same appetite. Although, the way he dressed up in that elf outfit at work, he might've had an inkling of a shared desire.

The fries arrived on the table for us to share. I dug in, they were freshly hot, but after my day, I needed something to munch on.

"When we head back to mine, I'll need to go in first, just to move some things around," he said, dipping his fries into ketchup.

I didn't mind what he had to do; I was just grateful for a place to stay.

THREE

KAMDEN

Maybe I shouldn't have drunk so much, but once we got talking, my lips became loose, and then suddenly, out of nowhere, I was telling this guy all about my art. I never meant to, but there was something in his dark eyes that told me I could trust him, and I was a sucker for something to suck on.

I'd supposed to go into the apartment before him to move things around, but that didn't happen. We were both drunk and high on Christmas cheer and spirit. We walked in together, laughing in each other's arms.

Everything was on show. My paintings. My art. My identity. As well as the small poorly decorated plastic

Christmas tree, sat on the coffee table.

Gage propped me up straight. "Oh."

"I—I should've moved everything before you came up."

The apartment wasn't a mess, but the view from the doorway told a different story.

There was a dust sheet on the ground. My easel, canvas, and a several bottles of paint. It wasn't that either that shocked him on arrival. It was the painting of a man, shirtless, trousers unbuckled, a hand wiping at his lip and saying. *'Come to Daddy.'*

"It's an art project," I blurted.

Gage kissed me. His hands on my jacket, unzipping it and pulling my arms out. "You can call me an art project."

I pressed my face deep against his, kissing him back. Maybe it was the adrenaline of someone catching my kink on canvas, or perhaps it was the alcohol. I couldn't think too much about it, my head was spinning with the alcohol running through me.

His hands down by my thighs, squeezing. I jumped on his hips, pushing his arms out of his jacket to undress him.

He took me to the sofa, sitting as my legs were around him, I sat on his lap.

"You're looking for a Daddy?" he moaned in my ear.

"Why?" I asked, catching my breath. "Do you think I've found one?"

Everything stopped. Our deep gazes connecting each other, and the way our breathing synced up. Our chests in rhythm.

"For tonight," he said. "You can call me Daddy."

I slammed my chest hard against his before our lips locked. His hands on my body, grabbing at my skin and clothes. I begged him to undress me.

"Say *please Daddy*."

"Please, Daddy."

Switching positions, he sat me on the sofa and started tugging at my trousers. He looked up ahead, behind me, staring at the canvas I'd been working on. "Good boy," he whispered. "Maybe you can paint me."

I placed my hands over my tight snowman print briefs and the boner inside. "You're not doing this so I'll let you sleep in my bed, are you?"

Gage pulled his t-shirt and vest up over his head, showing me the patch of hair on his chest. I was too distracted to focus on an answer. "I'm fine sleeping on the sofa, and fucking here too, if that's what you want?" he reached out, placing his thumb to my lip like the man on the canvas. "You do want to fuck, right?"

"Fuck me, Daddy" I let out in a breathy voice.

"Where's your limit?" he asked, moving his hand down from my mouth to my t-shirt. "What's your play? Rough, sweet, force?" His fingers explored over my t-shirt for my nipples. They were so sensitive in the cold, but I wanted his touch to warm them up.

"Control," I said, immediately. I knew what I wanted. I

wanted to surrender to another, to give them my body. "Take control of me."

He clicked his tongue. "Address me as Daddy, and I'll see what I can do."

"Control me, Daddy," I whispered.

This is what I'd been searching for, someone who knew how my body and mind operated, and then gave me what I wanted. Gage was gentle as his facial hair brushed against my torso, his mouth trying to find my nipples. Soft kisses woke large moans and my back to arch up into his face.

He reached around, hooking his arms together beneath my back and lifted me. "Be a good boy and show me how good you really are." I was on his knee now, in a whir of motion. He placed his thumb at my pouting lips once more, pushing them down for me to open my mouth. "That's right he said, it's better if you open up."

His hard cock was on my leg, throbbing for attention inside his briefs. I found myself on my knees seconds later, slipping between his legs and ready to devour his cock. It was the alcohol in me that woke this particular horny beast.

Pulling his briefs down, I was almost slapped in the face by his uncircumcised cock, the pink head stretching out the skin with the pre-lubricated precum. I glanced up at his smiling face, he reached out with a hand, placing it on my head as I went down on him, taking his cock in my mouth, tasting the precum on my tongue and at the back of my throat.

His head leaned back on the sofa; his mouth open wide as he moaned.

I hadn't given head in a while, but it was just like riding a bike, except, there was no chance of falling off, but one-hundred percent chance that an accident in my pants could happen if I continued. I tried not to play with myself as I sucked his cock, but it was hard, literally.

He pulled me up on the sofa and laid me out sideways. "I want to know what you taste like," he whispered in my ears before going down on me. I squirmed under the tickles of his touch, but then I stopped. His mouth around my cock was so warm and calming, even as my pulse raced, and I knew I was getting harder in his mouth.

"Ok, ok." I didn't know how long I would last in his mouth.

He looked up at me, a saliva trail from where his mouth and my cock were connected. "I want to taste you," he said. "Cum in my mouth." He gave my cock a couple tugs, staring deep into my eyes.

My thighs clenched and my toes curled.

"Are you ready?"

I was close. I couldn't vocalize it, only nod and moan.

He took my cock in his mouth and within seconds, the firework explosions popped inside me as I came to a climax. I felt his tongue on the tip of my cock, take in every single drop of cum down his throat.

In the post-nut haze and still quite drunk, I reached out

to pet his head. "Thank you, Santa."

"I'll never let protein go to waste," he said, his thick lips now cold as he kissed my cheek.

Stretching out my legs, I sighed. "I thought we were going to have sex."

"What makes you think we're not?"

My brows together, I stared into the abyss of warmth in his brown eyes. "Because I came." Looking at his body laid on mine, he lifted himself to show his cock still hard and ready to go, right beside mine which was now becoming soft. "But you didn't."

"That's right, if you want me to fuck you, all you have to do is ask."

"Is that one of your Santa wishes?" I asked.

"It's a wish I can grant," he whispered.

"In my room," I whispered back. "Take me to my bed first." I didn't have any intention of being fucked on my sofa, although there was a first for everything.

"So, this is how you get me in bed?" he snickered.

"No," I giggled. "You can go back to the sofa afterwards."

He lifted me up, teasing me like a mall Santa Daddy would, telling me I was about to go on the naughty list. I knew if that happened, I had tricks up my sleeve to help get me put back on the nice list.

My bedroom was through a door on the side wall. There were two doors, one to the bathroom, and a second to my bedroom. He was lucky, carrying me through to my room without tripping on anything in the process.

The room was lit from the light outside. It was Christmas and everywhere was decorated with colorful light.

On the bedside table, I noticed it before him, it was my pacifier. It was what I chewed on while I was painting, and sometimes I didn't take it out until I was already in bed. I grabbed it, holding it in a fist before he could see.

"What is it?" he asked.

I showed him.

"Adorable," he whispered. "So, what are you gonna do?" He took the pacifier from my hand. "Do you want it in your mouth? Or do you want to suck on something else?" He smacked a hand at his erection. It bounced, up and down. My eyes were fixed on it, up and down, left and right.

I grabbed it. "Mine."

"Good boy."

Gage rolled onto the bed, on his knees over my body, he pushed the cock in my face.

It was a gift, already unwrapped, and I was ready to receive it.

Sucking down as far deep as I could, deep throating it like candy would come out if I could get my nose pressed against his pelvis.

He pulled away. "You're gonna make me cum doing that. I thought you wanted me to fuck you."

"You're right," I said, half slurring. "Fuck me now." I

reached into the bedside drawer and pulled out a comically long string of condoms. It was a clear indicator of how underfucked I was.

He clicked his tongue, tutting at me. "I'm the one in control, remember. Surrender to Daddy."

If I wasn't reminded, I forgot, or perhaps that was because I was several cocktails deep.

Gage turned me over and gave my ass a gentle spank. "Oh, you're well stocked," he said.

"That's the cookies," I said, my face pressed into the pillow.

"I meant the lube in your drawer," he chuckled. "But your ass also looks stocked up and delicious."

I was ready to say something back, but before I could, the overwhelming pleasure of his mouth against my ass tingled through me. When I was younger, having my ass eaten gave me anxiety, but I was much more confident now, and I knew, even with the lack of dick in my life, to always be prepared to have my ass eaten, just in case I was getting an early Christmas wish.

"You like that?" he asked, taking a hand up and down my back scratching the surface. I took it as a cue to arch and press his face deeper. He took my ass by force, almost like it belonged to him. I was already hard again, I didn't know if that meant I'd be able to handle myself, or whether I'd cum a second time just as fast. His hand took my cock, pulling it down so he could suck it a second time.

"Fuck me," I begged, my hot face pressing harder into the pillow. It was almost like I was blindfolded, and now all my senses were on fire, and as soon as that fire came and consumed me, it vanished. His body removed from mine. Then his cock slapped against my hole. "Do it."

"Here," he whispered. "Put this in." His hand on my face, he stuffed my pacifier in my mouth. "I'll do what I want."

That's all I wanted. Being stuffed up by my pacifier, and then by something slender, like a finger, down to the knuckle. A second finger, and then—

"Moan if you enjoy it."

His cock, stretched my hole, going slow inside me. I moaned, the vibration of it came from my chest and echoed out.

He laid out on my back. A hug from the inside and out, his slow strokes were heaven. He grabbed both my hands, pinning them up above me. He moved to my legs, like a game of footsie, his legs grabbed mine and spread them. His cock seemed to go deeper, like he'd opened me up wider than I'd ever been before.

"Good boy." He kissed my neck and back, pulling away as his hands pressed down on my lower back, arching me. "That's right. This ass is mine."

It was his, I didn't disagree.

I felt the heat of his pulsating cock as he stopped thrusting. He came. Part of me wished he'd come bare inside me, filled me up like a Christmas pudding. But that wasn't safe.

He removed his cock slowly. I turned to see him, panting, sweat glistening in the light casting over him from outside. He flopped beside me on the bed.

Pushing the pacifier to the side of my mouth, I stared at him as he stared at the ceiling. "You can sleep in the bed," I said.

"That's a relief, actually," he said with a wide grinning smile. "Because I'm probably too tall to sleep on that sofa." He leaned in and kissed me. "We should probably clean off before bed."

"Is that your way of asking if you can use my shower?"

"It was actually my way of asking if you'd join me in taking a shower." He gave my ass a spank. "I wasn't asking for permission."

FOUR

GAGE

I never expected to fuck him. I never expected to fuck anyone. For a while it felt like I'd become celibate. Not because I didn't want to fuck, or because I didn't have people who wanted me to fuck them, but because I was thirty-four years old, and I knew what I wanted, I just didn't want to go through the talking stages of meeting someone new again, only to realize they weren't into the same things I was.

One of my greatest fears was to find a man and him ending up being part of one of those families that goes hiking. That was an absolute nightmare. I could hike, I could walk up a mountain, but it would be a cold day in hell if someone were to wake me up at six in the morning, excited like it was Christmas day with enthusiasm for a morning hike.

Today, I woke up with the excitement running through me like a kid on Christmas morning.

But Kamden wasn't in bed beside me.

My brain threw around the idea that last night didn't even happen, but of course it did. This wasn't my apartment. These sheets were soft, like silk, but breathable like cotton. And I was naked, which wasn't a big surprise since I usually overheated at night if I had clothes on, even something as simple as underwear.

I waited for a moment, trying to listen to any sign of life. The bedroom door was ajar, but I couldn't make anything out from the slither of light.

Kamden wasn't here.

Putting on the briefs and my vest top from yesterday, I wandered around his apartment. It was big. Mostly in an L-shape with the living area and kitchen. Then his bedroom, bathroom, and a small walk-in closet were tacked onto the shape. I hadn't seen much of the apartment last night, after we came in, I basically pounced on him, we fucked, we showered, and then we slept.

He'd mentioned his art yesterday, and another reason I'd been so quick to fuck him after I saw the art.

He was a little, or at least his art gave the impression he was a little. The pacifier in his bedroom gave it away. Being called Daddy in any setting stirred up something feral, but in the best possible way. I didn't want children in that sense, but I did want the power of being Daddy. It's something people didn't understand, so flings and relationships didn't last since my needs were not being met.

The apartment door opened as I was busy rifling through the painted canvas stacked against the wall.

"You've been busy," he giggled. He was wrapped up warm and tight inside his winter clothes.

He was talented. Everything had *Daddy* in some phrase on the art. "I think I'm supposed to say that to you," I said. "Your art is incredible. Do you draw still life or is it from online referencing, or—"

"Hold on," he said, presenting me with two to-go coffee cups. "Yours is the one on the left."

"We should talk about last night," I said, accepting the coffee. "And—where are the rest of my clothes?"

Kamden pulled away his winter coat and gloves. "Last night, that was incredible. And I'm down to go again, just give me a minute."

I sipped on the coffee. It was intense with zero sweetness. "And what time is it?"

"All your things are hung up," he said, gesturing to the coat hook by the door.

I must've been blind to not notice my coat. Kamden moved it to show my backpack there.

"I was going to wash your clothes, because I know you

told me yesterday you wanted to wash them, but I figured if I did that then—" he spoke fast and with his hands.

"That's ok," I interrupted him. "My shift starts at ten."

"Oh. It's like nine," he said, shrugging. "Surely, we could get something done before work." He looked at me, his pouting bottom lip and wide eyes.

"Those eyes would usually work on me, but I can't be late to work," I told him, approaching the coat hooks with my clothes on.

"Why?" he asked. "People will wait."

"It's important to be on time," I told him, handing him back the drinks as I got dressed. "And that Santa suit takes time already to put on. Plus, I don't want to get fired."

"Well, my dad manages the mall, so that's the only reason I'm there."

Somehow that news didn't surprise me. This apartment, that job, it all made sense now. "So, you're a spoiled little boy?" I asked.

"Spoiled, yes. Little, sometimes. Boy, only if you put good before it."

"Then let me be the hand that tames you," I said in a whisper. He grew closer to me. "Since I'm guessing you're my elf as some type of punishment."

He giggled, immediately, biting his lips together. He blushed. "How are you going to tame me?"

"I'm sure I'll think of something for tonight," I teased.

"Yes, Daddy Santa," he said, saluting me. "I take it that

means you'll be staying over again tonight."

"With some rules," I added.

"Rules?"

"Yeah. We can't get drunk like last night. And I need to do laundry. These are the only clothes I have," I told him. "At least until I can get back into my apartment." I dug a hand around in my backpack and pulled out a pair of socks. I knew to always have a spare pair of socks, especially in this weather, socks got soaked so easily.

"I'll drive us into work," he said. "Plus, my car looks nicer."

I cracked a smile, snickering at him. "Of course, it does, spoiled boy."

We made it to the mall, on time, which was late for me since I still had to go through the process of putting on the padding and then the Santa suit. I couldn't blame Kamden though; he was so adorably sweet. Plus, he was right, kids would wait for Santa, their parents would complain, but the world wouldn't crumble and burn because I was a couple minutes late.

Being Santa was fun, I got to sit down all day, listen to the magic of children's Christmas wishes and tell them they were all on the nice list. Kamden handed them their gift bag and then they went off with the magic of Christmas in their eyes. I could tell Kamden was growing tired though, which I understood since I was so used to standing around, walking up and down this mall in the heavy penguin mascot outfit.

"Can I sit on your lap?" he asked under his breath, hunching his shoulders and sighing.

"Maybe later," I said. "You need to keep letting them in. There's a line forming."

He grumbled. "Fine, but when do we break for lunch?"

"In thirty minutes," I told him.

I didn't know if that was true, someone came to me and told me when lunch was and when to take my breaks.

As lunch rolled around, and I'd expected to talk back in the break room with Kamden, but I realized he'd gone off on his own somewhere.

In the break room, there were baguette sandwiches already out on a fold out plastic banquet table. There were also snack foods as well. This wasn't usual, probably just something they were doing for the holidays, and I was thankful for it because I hadn't brought food, and I didn't want to get swamped by kids if I went to line up at some fast-food kiosk.

Armed with a beef, lettuce, and tomato baguette, I saw to eat and look through my phone.

Alexia had called several times already. I got my hopes up, thinking the apartment was fine.

"*No, I was just calling you to make sure you were sleeping rough,*" she said.

"I slept—"

"*Where?*"

Covering the speaker against my mouth, I couldn't exactly talk about it out in the open. "I slept with this guy I met yesterday."

"*And the dry spell is over,*" she cackled. "*I suppose when you're in need, the world truly does provide.*"

"Shhh, Alexia, seriously," I hummed. "He's really nice. He went out and got us coffees this morning. I didn't know if I'd wake up in *Misery* or not."

She continued to cackle down the phone as I told her about Kamden. She wanted all the details, like height, age, and how big his dick was. Our friendship had no limits, we knew everything about each other, even our kinks, which we found out one night after getting very wine drunk.

Sauntering into the break room with a square paper bag swinging on his arm, Kamden smiled, waving at me. I cut the call. Seeing him gave me flutters.

"So, I figured you're gonna be over for a few nights, and this might be totally overstepping, but I bought you a couple things," he said, pulling out clothes from the bag. "Pack of boxer briefs. Pack of—"

I held his hand before he could pull anything else out. "I—I'm super grateful for this."

"But you think I'm overstepping," he said.

"No, no, I mean, maybe a little, but no, I appreciate this."

Kamden looked around as I guided his eyes with mine. "Oh, the people," he mouthed.

"You're lucky I didn't come in and say what I was going to say," he snickered, sitting down at the table beside me. "Ew. Are we really eating this?" His nose wrinkled up as he looked to the half-eaten baguette.

"*We* aren't eating this, I am," I said, grabbing the end and stuffing it in my mouth.

"Wait," his voice turned soft. "You weren't going to share with me?" His brows creasing and his lips pouting.

I couldn't tell if this was an act, or whether he was really like that all the time. He changed when we were alone, so I assumed he was less pompous, but with still a light salting of sass. "I've got to keep my energy up," I said after swallowing. "I've got such a tough job."

"Let me tell you what else I got," he said. "It's nothing. Really. I had a gift card, and it was burning a hole in my pocket." He scoffed. "You know, my dad's basically forcing me to be an elf to make money, so I have to resort to using gift cards."

For a moment, I stared at him, up and down. "Do you ever listen to yourself?" I asked. "Like, when you say something, what does it sound like?"

"I know," he said, raising a brow at me. "I sound entitled." His energetic stance left his body as he seemed to deflate. "I'm not really like that, it's just—" And there it was, real and raw. He was letting his guard down.

I reached out and slipped my hand into his. "I like this version of you," I told him. "So, do you want some of my sandwich?"

He smiled. "I'll probably go see what they have left, I'm actually starving," he said. "Anyway, look in the bag, it's just a couple things."

Inside the bag, he bought me underwear, some vest tops, and a joke t-shirt that read '*my eyes are down here*' and an arrow pointing to the crotch. I had to give it to him, it was funny. I was also thankful the underwear wasn't covered in days of the week like some of his were.

With a sandwich and a chocolate muffin, Kamden sat at the table again. "I was thinking." He glanced around and lowered his head. "Does Santa want to take home a naughty elf tonight?" he whispered. "We should borrow these outfits."

"As long as you don't want me to take the padding under it," I said, shifting around, feeling at how stiff the stuffing had become around my limbs. "And thank you for the clothes. I guess now I'll need to get you something."

"I'll send you my Amazon wishlist."

I let out a chortle. "Whatever I get you, it'll be something I think of myself." And I already had an idea. Plus, it worked well with these outfits.

FIVE

KAMDEN

I wasn't the only person working at the mall as an elf. There were elves dressed up everywhere. Everyone wanted to work the Santa's grotto, but since it was a stationary position it meant my dad could keep an eye on it, and on me. He was really making me work for this money.

We were only halfway through work after lunch when my dad called me to his office. I thought I was a key player in the elf business, but someone slipped into my place as soon as I left to go see my dad.

"I'm having fun," I said in a strop.

He chuckled at me, taking his phone out and snapping a picture, with flash. It seemed like taking a picture with poor lighting should've been a crime. "Naomi decided she isn't quitting. I don't know what changed her mind. I guess she needs the money."

"I don't know who that is," I said, slumping into the chair across form his desk. "And what does that have to do with me?"

"Well, she was the elf working the grotto."

"Ok, and?"

"And I won't need you to work the grotto anymore," he said, smiling as if this was good news.

"No, no, I—"

"I thought you'd like that," he said. "I'm still gonna need you to work, we have leaflets that need hanging out, or I know you mom was looking around to hire some elves as stagehands for the town hall production this weekend."

"Absolutely not."

Even though I didn't really want to work the grotto, that's where Gage was working. I needed to flirt with him, I needed to look into his gorgeous eyes otherwise I'd melt, unable to do anything. He gave me energy to be an elf. I wouldn't be able to muster the same type of excitement if I was going to be an elf in the wild.

"What I'm saying is, I'm actually proud you've stuck it through," he said. "And we'll give it a couple more days, and you can have the money."

It was still partly about the money, but it wasn't completely about it. I'd got my one Christmas wish, and that was to have someone in my bed with me, a hot, handsome someone at that. The other part of my Christmas wishlist I could go without. A giant teddy, large enough to smother me if it was sentient.

"Fine, but I'm going back to the grotto to finish off being an elf for the day," I scoffed.

"Wait." He rubbed at his eyes. "I know what this is about. You've got a crush on the guy we've got playing Santa."

Stunned. It felt like I constantly kept him on his toes as a parent. In fact, I probably kept them both on their toes. Except, this time, he might've had me figured out, well, just a little bit, at least. "No comment," I rebuffed.

"Kam, I really don't need a HR headache," he groaned.

"It's consensual," I said.

I could see it in my father's face, the point of giving up. It happened regularly. "Fine, but please, don't do anything that could land either of us in hot water. And your mom also wants you to go visit her. You live across the road from the community center, please, go show your face once in a while."

"But dad, my art."

"*But dad, my art,*" he mocked, chuckling to himself. "She wants to see you. I've also sent her that picture I took of you on the way in. Maybe show up in the elf costume for her."

That was an idea I could get behind, not the showing up

in the elf costume, but the permission to take it out of the mall. "I'll think on it."

"Don't think too hard," he teased.

I loved my parents to bits, and they loved me. They supported everything I did. The apartment I was living in had been the first apartment they bought together. Then they had me, rented the apartment out until I graduated college, and I put my foot down and told them I wanted my own space to do my art in. Plus, the light through the apartment was impeccable. It was a shame I wasn't there right now making the most of the natural light and the striking inspiration I'd been collecting ever since Gage laid me down on that bed and stuffed my face into the pillow.

Since there was already an elf helping Gage play mall Santa, I took a round trip around the mall. I helped myself to hot chocolate and something to curb my sweet tooth. I took a lap around the grotto, trying to catch Gage's eye, and I did, but then his new elf friend got in the way of our deep and meaningful connection.

He was my Santa.

The needy inner child was coming out.

And I didn't share, at least, I didn't want to share, not with any other elf.

I waited in the changing room for Gage to finish. I'd already changed and stuffed the elf outfit inside a plastic bag to take home with me.

My mom had called a bunch, as had Sian from the local

gallery. *The Hinton Gallery*. Sian was probably my closest friend in town, and the only friend I'd stayed close to since graduating from college together.

"Hi hon," Sian answered. "Dodging my calls?" she snickered.

"No, I've been busy."

"Well, I hope you've been busy working on something for me," she said. "You know I've got a couple of spots open for you in the spring. It's been over a year since we had that abstract piece. I'm desperate to get another one."

In the uninspiring fluoresce of the changing room, I couldn't help feelinig so completely uninspired by everything around me. "I might have found a muse," I told her. "But I don't know."

"Come in and speak to me about it," she said. "Better yet, I'll see you on Saturday at the Christmas fair. I want to talk about the talent I'm showcasing this spring."

There was no escaping that, I was living directly above the festivities. "Maybe I can show off my new muse," I giggled. It came out of nowhere; the childish excitement had fluttered up through my stomach.

"I look forward to it."

I hung up, knowing full well I shouldn't have been putting so much pressure on the way Gage made me feel. This was temporary, like a season, it would go like melted snow soon enough. But that didn't mean I couldn't enjoy jumping in and making snow angels while the snow was falling.

Gage came into the changing room, sighing with the weight of the Santa padding. He was followed in by others dressed in their elf costumes. I tried not to give any of them the stink eye, but it was practically impossible to control my facial expression once it had made its mind up.

He rested against the lockers like he was some high school jock. "So, I've got something for us later," he said. "And by later, I mean when we're back at yours," he whispered, extending a hand, he pressed his thumb at my bottom lip. "Stop pouting."

Pouting was also another feature of my resting face. And I found it adorable. "Well, can you get changed quick so we can leave. I also *might* have a surprise." I didn't, but I knew the excitement of a surprise might encourage him to hurry a little.

It worked. He was ready to go and had stuffed his Santa suit without the beard into his bag to take with us.

"Where did you go today?" he asked as we walked out in the dark, snowy parking lot.

"My dad told me I wasn't going to be working with you anymore."

"Oh." He paused me, placing his hand on mine. "Any reason why?"

"The girl who quit, she's not quit anymore. Whatever that means." I rolled my eyes.

"Hey," he said. "Is that why you've been sulky?" He

smiled. His cheeks pinching into dimples. "I mean, I saw you walk by a couple times, and you looked like you were about to throw your hot chocolate over someone."

"I'm sorry. I'm usually better at hiding my feelings."

He tucked his hand into mine. "I don't believe that for a single second. And I missed you not being up there. But I don't want you to be in a mood over it."

He was right. I was getting eaten up over nothing. "Why does it sound so reasonable coming from you?"

"Because I'm the voice of reason, clearly," he chuckled. "You know, you've inspired me. Maybe I can take some pictures of you later."

"Only if I can draw you."

He squeezed my hand, pulling me into his arms. He kissed me, his cold nose pressing against my cheek.

I was being swept away, and I didn't care. He could take me all the way out to sea, as long as he was with me.

In my car, blasting the heaters and getting the ice from the windows, I caught Gage glancing at me.

"Do you think this would've ever happened?" he asked.

"Maybe," I said. "I hope. I probably wouldn't have invited you to move into my apartment so quick."

"Beneath that sassy exterior, I can see you're just a soft boy." He pulled his glove away and placed his hand on my cheek. His skin was warm. I leaned into his touch. "When we get back to your place, I don't know if I'll be able to keep my hands off you."

"Sounds like a promise," I said, presenting my pinky finger out to him.

As soon as we got back to the apartment, Gage was true to his word. His hands clung to my skin, removing all my clothes in the process. We started out against the wall, and up against the window, my bare cheeks pressed against glass, imprinting them like a calling card.

Out of breath, we were both on the floor, almost in the mess of paint.

Gage stood. "On your knees," he instructed. "Want me to get the Santa suit out?"

"Yes, Daddy."

It was a very quick change of clothes, slipping on his Santa trousers, the hat, and wearing the jacket like a loose unzipped coat, showing off his hairy body.

"Where's your elf hat?" he asked. "Put it on like a good little elf boy."

I did as he instructed, alongside the red and white striped tights I had been wearing under my elf suit. The hat and tights made for a sexy elf.

"Look how obedient you're being," he said. "Do you like being obedient?"

He knew the answer, but as I regressed back to my little space, I knew the correct answer would get me a reward. "Yes, Daddy." I nodded.

"Good elf. Now, close your eyes and open wide," he said. "Santa's got to empty his sack somewhere."

Eyes screwed shut, mouth open, tongue out. I waited.

Something sweet entered my mouth. I opened wider. It wasn't his dick. I'd just been sucking that, and as hard as it was, it was a rock. My tongue explored it, tasting the sugary sweetness. There was peppermint to it. I knew then, it was a candy cane.

"You like that?" he asked, stroking a thumb under my chin. "You want to take more of it?"

There was no way I'd be able to answer, my jaw was opened as wide as it could go with the candy in my mouth. I let out a gargled muffle of a response.

"Open your eyes," he said.

At waist level, right where his dick should've been, there was a candy cane. A delicious surprise. And at least there wouldn't be any complaints if my teeth touched it.

He pulled it from my mouth. "Give it a good suck," he said. "I want to see where I can put it."

Immediately, my eyes lit up. And as the obedient little elf, looking for his reward, I gave that candy cane the biggest slurp and suck as I could possibly.

We moved to the sofa where I laid across his lap, my ass in the air. I continued to keep the large candy cane in my mouth as he parted my cheeks, squeezing them and giving tender spanks. They were reward spanks, like he was getting me ready for the pounding of a lifetime.

He pulled the candy cane from me and slowly inserted it inside my ass. It was stretching me out. I moaned, begging for him to go a little deeper with it. He pulled it out and went to town, eating my ass, licking at all the stickiness around my hole.

"You like that?" he asked.

"Again, again!"

I wasn't sure which part I enjoyed more, the part where he shoved it inside me, or the part where his tongue explored the sweetness stuck to my skin.

There were no wrong moves between us. Usually there was a constant worry I was doing something wrong, but Gage didn't let any of those worries surface, not even for a moment. We shared one goal, motivated by our erections for each other.

It didn't last long until he had my head on his lap. He rubbed the candy cane on his cock, and I sucked it all off.

"I want it in my mouth," I said, sticking my tongue out. "Cum."

He chewed on his bottom lip, biting down.

"Pweese."

He'd been withholding it for as long as he could from me, but as soon as I told him I wanted it, he exploded in my mouth like a gushing candy tainted by the peppermint stickiness, I swallowed all of it, and I continued to work him to try to get more, but once the hardness went down, it was almost like sucking on a gummy worm.

His chest was going up and down, panting and grinning. "I wish I could've given you more," he whispered. "I want yours now."

SIX

GAGE

Everything about this was unlike me. Jumping into bed with someone I barely knew but trusted completely. We slipped into something together. My body, mostly slipping into his, again and again until our bodies grew tired, and the sun began to rise. I didn't even care, I'd survive on coffee and whatever pheromones Kamden was putting out in the air.

I woke before him. He laid still, so sweetly on the bed, sucking hard on the pacifier in his mouth. I traced a hand down his back, stopping at the sheet covering his juicy ass.

My camera was on the bedside table. I didn't think twice, I grabbed it and started snapping pictures of him and the way the light hit his body. It kissed his skin. The sunlight contrasting to the cold of winter. I continued to walk around the bedroom with my eye in the viewfinder, snapping picture after picture. Then I stubbed my toe, and of course, woke Kamden from his slumber.

"You take anything good?" he asked in a giant yawn, followed by deep stretches.

"You also promised you'd draw me," I said.

I joined him on the bed again, wrapping our bodies together for warmth. He hugged his head to my chest. "Aren't we going to be late for work?" he grumbled.

Not what I'd expect to come from him. From what I gathered; a day job wasn't something he was built for. Kamden was built for cuddles and being treated like a prince. I stroked his face. "We have a little while longer."

"Yesterday, you said being on time was late." His voice muffled as his face was pressed against me.

"Who are you trying to impress?"

"I just—I want to make sure I work with you, and I'll— and I'll—" he yawned, interrupting himself. "And I'll fight whoever I have to."

"I hope there's no fighting involved," I cooed. "First, shower, then breakfast, coffee, and work."

He cuddled himself harder against me, almost trying to become part of me by means of osmosis. "Ugh, I don't want to see my dad," he groaned. "I told him I'd see my mom yesterday, and—I totally didn't."

"You can see her today," I told him.

In a short amount of time, we'd created a nice connection with each other. It supported my idea that having sex with someone sped the emotional bonding process. And we'd bonded.

Today was a long day at the mall, it was the last night of late-night shopping. It meant I was about to be sat down a whole lot as I deepen my voice and tell everyone their Christmas wishes were going to come true. The Santa who did this before me had the look, the action, and the voice down. I was making it up as I went along, and looking back, I'm sure the illusion would be shattered for some kids.

Kamden and his coffee were inseparable. I didn't know how many espresso shots were in his cup, but he was sipping on it and wincing with each drink at the bitter taste. I'd taken a single sip of it and felt like I could see sounds and taste colors.

Before I got into the Santa suit, I had other plans involving a trip to the candy store, *Sugar High*. I knew the manager there, Riggs, he'd usually come by and give me a couple candies whenever I was in the penguin costume.

"Hey," Riggs said. "You're looking different."

Sugar High was an emporium of sweets. It's where I'd got the thick candy cane from yesterday. I wasn't planning on getting another, Kamden had barely sucked the first layer off it. It was splashed in neon colors at all corners, not ideal for someone with the attention span of a pigeon.

"Not in the Santa suit yet," I said. "Hopefully won't be

in it much longer, I prefer being the mascot and burning calories on my feet."

He chuckled. "So, what brings you in so early?"

There was a younger guy beside Riggs, grinning to himself and swaying back and forth, occasionally bumping hips with him.

"I'm actually looking for some lollipops, different sizes, flavors, that type of things," I said. "I want a selection.

Riggs presented the worker at his side. "If you need help, Tomas is my best employee."

"Is that all he is?" I asked, winking at him.

Riggs couldn't control his smile. "Maybe we can go for a drink some time and I'll—tell you all about it?"

Tomas stared at Riggs. "All?"

"Right, I need to get back to my job," Riggs said, giving Tomas's arm a squeeze. "Help Gage."

I walked around the store with Tomas.

"Riggs is a nice guy," I said.

"He's really sweet," he mumbled. "So, we have all of these, and we also have different shaped ones too, like, heart shapes, Christmas trees, and stuff." He presented the entire shelf to me.

I didn't press him on the Riggs thing. Riggs was a nice guy, but I knew he had a thing for the quiet twinky guys. "I'm actually just looking for just regular circles," I told him. In a way, I was hoping to use them in a similar way we'd used the candy cane last night. Lollipop anal beads came to mind, but I doubt I'd find anything like that here.

I grabbed a selection of sizes and flavors before paying and rushing back to the changing room to see Kamden already in his elf outfit, looking so damn adorable. He was talking to his dad. I almost backed out of the room to wait for them to finish.

"Gage," his father said, pulling me in. "I was just telling Kam that the old Santa is coming back tomorrow, so you'll be back on mascot duty."

"Right." I clutched the bag of sweets to my chest, trying to hide them from Kamden. "Well, I was actually scheduled in to take some time off."

"You are?" Kamden blurted before his father could.

"Sure. Was it approved?"

"Yep, but I was called in to do Santa," I said.

"Wait, so you weren't even supposed to be here?" Kamden continued.

I didn't know who I was having a conversation with at this point. "It was just a week," I said. "So, I'd like there to be a note about the days I actually worked."

His father jotted something down on the pad he held in his hand, cradled it like a baby's head to keep either me or Kamden from seeing what he was writing. "I'll make sure of that," he said. "So, you should be getting ready. I don't want a line of children and parents complaining about waiting. This isn't an amusement park," he scoffed.

As I dressed in the padding and then the Santa suit,

Kamden interrogated me about the time off I'd requested.

"I was going to use it as a time to get some photographs taken," I told him. "I've saved enough now to have a couple quality photos put on canvas. And I've got some great opportunities coming up."

"So, what you're saying is—" he paused, his eyes turning to squints as he looked at me. "It was fate that you were called in to play Santa the other day. And even more fate that I was forced into playing your elf."

In a room where people were coming in and out, it was hard to not take him against a locker. "You love being my little elf," I whispered, going closer to his face. "Play your cards right, and I'll make you a very happy elf."

"With that thing you were holding?" he asked. "What was it?"

"A surprise," I told him. "Now, we need to head out or I think your father might actually fire me."

He scoffed. "Over my dead body. I'd fight him before I'd let him fire you."

I gave his cheek a pinch. "You're cute when you frown like that." His cheeks a little pink, they added to the elf complexion.

I was impressed by Kamden's dedication to being my elf, and the effort he'd put. But then I saw how annoyed he looked when it came out that today was my last day as the Santa here. Although I knew that he'd just as easily quit being an elf.

The last late night of shopping at the mall, and it was hectic. I was glad not to be part of any of the people rushing around or lining up to meet *me*. I only had my mom and my grandma to buy for. My mom had been texting me for the past week, she was getting curious about my Christmas plans. It was difficult, my mom moved to Connecticut to live with her new husband a couple years ago, and my grandma stayed up here in Hinton at a local assisted living facility. I visited her when I could, and I'd visit her for Christmas to give her a gift.

"You know, I'm gonna need a massage later," Kamden whispered as one kid left my lap and he was getting ready to let another in. "I'm being serious," he grumbled.

"Ho, ho, ho—sounds like a great idea," I said in my deep voice.

"Ugh. There are people I know here." He pouted.

The Santa suit was a disguise. I saw an old high school friend appear with their children. Sometimes I forgot I was in my thirties and people my age had actual children. I didn't ever want children. As soon as they started crying, that was my cue to ship them back off to their parents. And children cried a lot, but that might've had something to do with being forced to sit on a stranger's lap after being threatened all year that Santa was always watching.

I knew Kamden wanted a massage after being on his feet all day, but I think I probably needed one just as much, if not more.

Neither of us wanted to move much after it was over. We struggled to get changed, a mixture of the tiredness creeping up on us and the work we'd done.

"I still have to go see my mom," he grumbled through a yawn. "I wanted to—" he paused, looking around. "To draw you."

"You did?"

My energy levels were replenishing at the idea that Kamden was going to draw me. "I guess I can give you something to stay awake for then," I said.

"Do I have to go see my mom first?" he grumbled.

Through his tired face, I could tell it was a serious question. "I think your dad wanted you to see her," I said. "Isn't it too late to visit?"

He shook his head. "Nope, she stays super late." He placed a hand over his mouth to yawn. "But I'm not coming in tomorrow, if you're not coming in, then I'm not either."

"Kam," I whispered. "You don't want to leave your dad understaffed."

"He's not," he said. "Trust me. I know."

My mind was already so tired, I didn't even know what we were talking about.

"Let's go to the break room and make espresso shots before we go," he suggested.

I understood espresso. He was speaking my language.

SEVEN

KAMDEN

Once we were back in the town center, freshly caffeinated and telling each other we'd never get any sleep now. I took a trip to the community center to visit my mom. She was still there, and all she wanted was to see my face. Which apparently was looking flushed. I didn't even need to tell her about Gage because my dad already had. I didn't know he was surveilling me at the mall, or maybe just making sure I wasn't going to become an HR disaster for him.

I was quick to get back to my apartment. Gage was already there, and I had hopes he would've been laid naked, ready and waiting to reward me.

The first half of my wish was granted.

Opening the door, Gage had rotated the sofa around. He laid on it, his elbow propping his head up. He smiled at me. His smile, the only distraction away from his half-naked body. "You told me you wanted to draw me."

"I did—I do!" My canvas and easel were ready in front of him. Kicking off my boots and pulling away my winter coat, I stood in front of the canvas. "You can't fall asleep while I'm doing it though."

"You'll just have to keep me talking," he said. "What do you want to talk about?"

"What's your favorite color?" I asked. We'd fucked, and I didn't even know his favorite color. I undressed until I was standing in front of the easel in my t-shirt, boxer briefs, and socks.

"Deep orange," he answered immediately. "Not neon, not bright, but you know when the sun is setting, and the sky goes dark. That's my favorite color."

"Ok, so you're a sucker for the golden hour," I said, looking him over. I grabbed my pencil, prodding the end to judge the sharpness. "My favorite color is this." I lifted my hand, wrist out. "That shade of blue. It's nice."

"Your veins?" he asked.

"Yeah," I giggled. "It's a good color. Plus, it's *my* color, so it has to be."

"I can't argue with that."

"Just need one more thing before I can begin." I rushed off to my bedroom, almost tripping myself up on the paint out on the dust cover.

Before I could begin any piece, I needed my pacifier. My little side was where I tapped my creativity. It stopped me from overthinking things and enjoying everything. My little side was responsible for some of my better abstract work as it forced me to put emotion on canvas raw.

For Gage, as he'd whirl winded his way into my life, I wanted something different. I could do people and places; it was all part of the college degree I earned.

Sticking the pacifier in my mouth, I looked directly at Gage's smiling face, and then back to the canvas. I grabbed a pencil and stared at it, almost trying to listen for its instruction.

I pressed the side of the pencil to the canvas, I lightly shaded out his body in shapes. That's all anything was when you reduced it down. Everything was a simple shape, and further, just a line. That's how I usually started. I liked to make sure there was just a touch of pencil on the canvas to lay out proportion and surroundings.

"How do I look?" he asked, pre-emptively.

"Good," I replied, my voice garbled behind the pacifier.

I wished we'd started this another time, but I wanted to immortalize him on canvas sooner. There was no telling how long this would last.

Once the pencil laid out on the canvas, I treated it like a blueprint. I went in with a base layer of white and yellow ochre, heavily diluted together to give the canvas a light, yet deep translucent yellow tone. The pencil stayed on the canvas as I applied the color. I hated painting on white canvas, there was nothing inspiring to it in my eyes. Too pure in some ways.

Glancing over at Gage, his eyes were closing. I'd been feeling the same way, but the sudden strike of creative inspiration was taking me for a ride. Painting to me was like blowing dust from something old. The first time you blow on it, a bit of what's behind is revealed, and the more you blow and dust away at it, the more features you see.

With a thick brush, I gave big strokes of stone blue to the background, each one a thin layer. It was the first blow to build that out, then came another blow, and another. And before I knew it, I'd fleshed out Gage's body, testing out skin colors and tones against my own skin. I was covered in it, up my arms from where I'd wiped the palette knife.

Gage stretched on the sofa, cracking his knuckles and yawning. "How long was I asleep for?"

Time moved different when my eyes were on canvas. It could've been years, but by the progress I'd made, I'd estimate a couple hours. The color profiles were built out, but this was in no way finished, and I wasn't going to let him peek or see it until it was completed.

"You can't see it," I said, pushing the pacifier to the corner of my mouth.

He stood, the boner in his briefs sticking out like it wanted attention. "Can I just take a peek?"

"Not even a peek." I held a finger up at him, still distracted by the bulge.

"Ok," he said. "Well, we should get you all cleaned up. I'm not sure if you have more paint on you or the canvas."

I shrugged. "And you'll never know," I teased. "Ok, I suppose when it's finished, you'll see."

Gage led me through to the bathroom. My limbs were already asleep on me. I didn't know how much longer I would be upright and awake.

"You know," Gage let out, yawning. He opened his mouth wide; I couldn't resist my inner voice as I told me to shove my finger in there. I pushed two fingers in his open mouth and then removed them, giggling to myself. "Tastes like—paints," he chuckled, smacking his tongue against the roof of his mouth.

"I couldn't resist it," I said before wrapping my paint covered body against his. I squeezed hard, making sure he was just as much covered in paint as I was. "Now, you'll have to shower with me."

He pulled the pacifier from my mouth and kissed me. "I hope you didn't think I was going to let you shower alone," he said. "And what I was about to say before you shoved two fingers in my mouth, was that I bought some lollipops earlier. I was thinking we might use them to play around with again. But maybe another time. I think this erection is the last of my energy."

"Then we shouldn't let it go to waste." My hand dug

down into his underwear and grabbed his dick. It bounced and throbbed in my palm.

He reached down at mine, but in my state of tired, I probably couldn't even summon the energy to get a boner, even if it usually seemed to pull from an energy reserve from elsewhere.

Gage undressed me from my t-shirt and tight teddy bear print underwear, getting me ready for the shower, while I didn't want to part with his cock. I held it, squeezing it and tossing as much and for as long as I could. It was clearly a distraction technique, a diversion while he got me into the shower.

Body wash and shampoo suds coated both our bodies. The steam from the hot water misting the space between us.

As he washed at the drying paint from my body, I was busy using the soap as lube to toss his cock. I could tell he was trying not to give in and cum with the way he shuffled back and forward, tensing himself.

"What reward are you trying to get?" he asked, stepping under the showerhead to wash the suds off his body.

Pouting, I stayed with my bottom lip until he opened his eyes again. "The one from your dick."

"Go on then," he said, resting his back against the tile. "Take it."

He turned the shower off as I got on my knees. I found the way his skin tasted odd since it had been washed with the soap. It was lacking a certain flavor. It didn't matter, dick was dick, and I enjoyed sucking on his dick like one of the lollipops he hadn't given me. I worked the head with my mouth and the balls with a hand.

It didn't take him long to bust his nut into the back of my throat.

I swallowed it all. Every drop I could get from his tip.

"Good boy," he said, looking down at me. He used his thumb to wipe my bottom lip. "I think that's all I've got left in me."

And now, it was all I had in me.

Sharing a big, fluffy towel, we dried each other off. Our fingers and eyes still in exploration mode. There wasn't a part of his body that I was bored of seeing. Even his hands, they were magical, more so because of how they made me feel when they were all over my body. My fingers traced the veins from his hands, up his arms, all the way to his chest.

I pulled his hand, wanting to go to bed.

"We need to brush our teeth," he said. "I guess you really do need me."

I really did need him.

We climbed into bed, naked and even after telling each other how tired we were, we still managed to waste time staring into each other's eyes and talking about our plans for the upcoming week. Sleep deprivation always brought out the inhibitions in me. And suddenly, I was saying things like.

"I don't think I need family for Christmas, I've got you."

And then before either of us could unpack that, my

eyelids were far too heavy to keep from closing and I was asleep.

EIGHT

GAGE

My phone woke me. At first, I tried to ignore it and go back to sleep. Kamden had coiled his body around mine. One arm over my torso, his legs around mine, and his head on my chest.

The second time my phone rang, I picked it up to see it was my mom.

She didn't usually call, so I answered. Pushing it to my ear and trying to be quiet.

"Everything ok?" I whispered. "Is it grandma?"

"*Surprise!*" her voice shrieked down the phone. "*I was going to surprise you at your apartment, but there's tape on the door. What's going on? Where are you?*"

"You should've told me you were coming to town," I said, trying to peel myself away from Kamden. "Where are you now?"

"Well, David is driving us up to visit grandma," she said. *"Maybe you want to come with us and grab some breakfast, then we can head to the Christmas fair."*

Of course, she never missed the Christmas fair. I should've realized. I'd been too busy with my time thinking about Kamden and being with him. "Let me get dressed and I'll drive up to meet you," I continued whispering.

"Where are you going?" Kamden groaned, trying to cling hold of me as I slipped out of bed.

"See you then sweetie," she said before hanging up.

I sat on the edge of the bed and stroked Kamden's face. "I'm going to meet my family. Well, mom, stepdad, and grandma."

"You want me to come with you?" he asked, rubbing his sleepy eyes.

Kissing his forehead, I contemplated falling back into the warmth of his body in bed. "I'll introduce you later," I said. "Get some more sleep, and maybe see if you can help out at the fair."

Pouting, he sighed. "I suppose I can do that."

"Good, because then when I introduce you to my family, they'll see you as adorable and helpful." I gave him another kiss.

He grabbed my arm, trying to keep me beside him. "Are

you saying I'm not helpful?"

"No, I'd never say something like that, but you did say you weren't helpful, even though you made an excellent elf," I said.

"That's very true." He yawned, stretching his limbs and letting me go. "And don't even dare look at the painting yet. I'll be so mad if you do."

My smile grew, looking at his feisty face. "If that's your mad face, then I'm tempted to see it again," I said. "Cutie."

"We're doing pet names?" he asked.

"Well," I began, cocking my head to look at him. "You do call me Daddy." And I was trying to be a positive guide. He needed it, and since spending time with him, I had seen a shift in his behavior. The reward he was looking for had been sex, and it worked both ways for the both of us.

I got dressed in the doorway for him to watch me, his eyelids fluttering back as I watched him find peace in sleep. I gave him a kiss on the forehead before leaving.

My mom's sudden appearance wasn't exactly sudden, but I didn't think she'd make it up this year. I figured I'd call in on my grandma over the weekend, and then the apartment fiasco happened, and it felt like I put life on pause. Of course, life did anything but pause for me.

Scraping the ice from my car window, I could see people setting up for the fair. There was a bakery in town that made these divine gingerbread cheesecakes. I remembered my mom buying one last year. We ate it at my apartment over

Christmas dinner, that was when Alexia had volunteered since her folks had gone on a cruise that year.

Blasting the heat and my music, still living in my teen era as pop punk music pumped through the speakers. It was great music to get amped and energized.

The assisted living facility in Hinton was almost a small village. It was a place where the elderly went to live once they couldn't live alone but still wanted independence. They had their own on-site store, cafe, and restaurant. The roads and sidewalk in and around the area never had a lick of snow on them, but they were constantly covered in salt grit to keep it from happening.

It seemed a popular choice for families to visit today. The cafe was full of people, my family included. I was late, but my mom had ordered me a double shot of espresso. It almost felt like a requirement. My mom, a complete heart of gold. She squeezed me in tight with a hug and made a comment about how good I smelled.

"I heard about the apartment," grandma said, shaking her head. "You should've come and stayed with me. The idea that you're out there in some random place during the holidays make me worried." She shook her head at me.

"Grandma, you know I can't stay over."

"Mom, you don't exactly have the space."

She scoffed at the both of us.

David smiled, looking for a moment to say something it seemed.

"Where are you two staying?" I asked before getting my first buzz of caffeine. "I was looking for hotels, but everything is booked up, and overpriced."

Mom pawed at the table. Her fingernails were decorated in deep red with gold flourishes. "We've had this booked for months," she said. "I thought you knew. And if you need a space to stay, we can get a rollout cot for the room back at the hotel."

"I'm staying with a guy I know from work," I said, it was technically the truth.

"That's nice," David added. "Your mom was telling me about a gallery showing."

"I'm just talking to someone who runs a gallery here," I said. "But I think they'll be showing some of my photography this spring."

"I hope I'm invited," Grandma said. "And if you need me to put in a good word with anyone here, let me know. These walls are packed with wealthy people." She whispered, growing closer to the table, her eyes shifty as she looked from left to right. "I'm working on commission."

I loved my grandma. She was supportive, sometimes too supportive.

"And you're still working as the mall mascot, right?" David asked.

"I just did a couple days playing Santa. I have some pictures on my phone, you're not gonna recognize me," I said, pulling my phone out. I suddenly became conscious of what might appear if one of them took my phone and they just started swiping. "In fact, I'll just texted it to you so you can have it." Crisis averted.

After coffee and breakfast, talk turned to the Christmas fair. My grandma's eye lit up. She'd been going to the fair for years. She once told me she'd been going since she was a girl, but I wasn't sure how accurate that was, since I think they'd only been running the Christmas fair for the last fifteen years.

I was excited to visit the Christmas fair with my family, and hopefully Kamden's there helping, but if not, then I knew he'd probably be up in the apartment working on the painting. Although I would've preferred it if he'd helped, I knew it would've been appreciated.

My mom and stepdad drove grandma, and I drove alone, but that meant I got to call Kamden, because there was something niggling in the back of my head that he might've just decided to stay in bed and do nothing until I got back.

"*Hey, are you coming back for cuddles?*" he answered.

There was background noise, so now I was unsure. "What did you get up to when I left?"

He groaned. "*I went to help my mom, my dad texted me telling me that if I wasn't going to be an elf, I could at least give my mom a hand making up gift bags.*"

"Then you'll definitely get some cuddles when I'm back," I said. "I'm on my way now, where will I find you?"

"*Wait, what?*"

"Yeah, they took my mom's car, you're on loudspeaker."

"*You're all coming here now?*" he asked, his voice growing quiet. "*But I haven't even properly got dressed. I'm in my sweats. Oh my god. Mom!*"

"Kam, Kam, it's—"

"*I'll see you when you get here!*" he cut the call.

Perhaps it was a good idea to warn him then, I knew my family wouldn't care if he wore sweats or clothes covered in paint. I always remember my mom and dad sitting me down and telling me they didn't care who I loved, as long as I was happy. I think they always knew I was gay, in the typical way parents knew; I put my action figures up in some very peculiar positions, and it was those very positions I continued to use today.

I hadn't counted on the roads being closed off for the fair, which meant I had to walk five minutes from where I'd parked to get to the town center. My family were already there, walking around in the bustle of the event. The smell of deep-fried foods and coffee welcomed me. It had the smells of a carnival without all the production value.

Riggs and Tomas were there, holding hands. I gave Riggs a knowing wink.

Kamden had texted me with his location, he was handing out winter mittens to people who needed them.

My mom stood right in front of him.

"I see you've met my mom," I said, trying to get introductions out of the way.

Grandma was busy looking at the gloves, removing hers for a brand-new pair. "You don't mind, do you?"

"They're yours to take," Kamden said with a wide smile. "And hi."

"Kamden," I said. "Mom. This the guy who is letting me crash at his place for a few days."

From behind Kam, a loud squeal came. A woman with dark graying hair appeared. "So, you're the reason my son has been helpful today," she said. "His dad mentioned him having a crush."

"Mom," he grumbled, stomping a foot on the wet ground. "I—"

"Well, I guess we are dating," I blurted. I didn't know if it was the right move to make, but to put aside any of the growing blush on Kamden's face, I was willing to move our situationship forward.

It was followed with Kamden's father, my boss, arriving with a chicken leg in his hand and a paper napkin tucked into his collar. "I guess the surprises keep coming," he chuckled. "Hi, I'm Kamden's father."

My stepdad reached out to shake his hand. Kamden's father raised his hand up, showing the drumstick. "You should grab one of these," he said. "Absolutely divine. The butcher and one of the chefs from the restaurant teamed up. They've got a hog roast going as well."

At the mention of a hog roast, my stomach rumbled.

"I won't be able to have any of that, not unless someone

plans on blending it up for me," Grandma said, chuckling loudly to herself.

"So, Gage," Kamden's mom, almost forwardly addressing me in the center of attention. "Maybe you can persuade Kam into showing us some of his art. He's so secretive."

"Gage is just as secretive," my mom blurted. "He's got some gallery thing happening in the spring and he hasn't shown us a single photograph in months. You know, Gage took this gorgeous landscape a couple years ago. I've still got it in the hallway at home, people are always asking who took it like I got it from some famous photographer." She cackled, swotting my arm. "One day though, son. One day."

As my mom spoke, Kamden glared at me, cogs turning behind his eyes. "The gallery," he said. "You know Sian?"

"Yeah, do you?"

"We went to college together."

"Well, it looks like our lovebirds have flocked together," my mom said, still snickering.

Kamden was excused from work to enjoy the Christmas fair with me.

Something about our families meeting had my heart pounding out of my chest. It wasn't that I was nervous about them meeting, it was more because of how new me and Kamden were. You couldn't label something this new, unless it was just labeled that. New.

We walked around, our gloves off as we held hands to

keep them warm.

"It's going to feel weird when your apartment is ready," he said. "You know—" He turned his head away.

"It'll be fine," I told him. "I know where you live, and you'll know where I live, and even if I don't tell you, I'm sure you'll find some way to get that address from your dad."

He squeezed his lips together into a devilish thin smile. "I wouldn't, but now you've put it in my head. You're a bad influence."

"What were you going to say?"

There was something distant in his eyes, like he was trying to figure out what was going to happen between the two of us after this period of being thrown together was over.

"Don't laugh, ok," he said.

"I'd never."

"So, my family gives me money each week to live on, it's for like food, and art supplies. They're like the best family I could ever wish for," he said, unable to hold eye contact. "When I want some extra money, or I charge my dad's credit card with something, they ask me to help out, either at the mall or the community center."

"Ok, that's no bad," I said. "I love that they support you, I wish my family did the same, but I do love putting on that mascot suit."

"That's not what I wanted to tell you." His grip on my

hand tightened. "I saw an advertisement online for this huge bear, life size, almost. I'm sure. Anyway, I kinda gave up on finding someone to be with, and I wanted something to share my bed with. A life size teddy bear was the solution to that."

It was sweet. "So, what are you saying?"

"I still want a giant teddy," he revealed. "And they—they have a Skee-ball game over there and if you get like a certain number of tickets, you can win a giant teddy bear."

Cupping a hand under his chin, I guided his face to mine. "Let's go win you a bear, but that doesn't mean I don't want to share your bed as well," I told him. "You can be sandwiched between me and the teddy." I gave him a kiss on his cold lips. "We should also get something warm to drink."

"Is it too early for mulled wine?" he whispered, batting his eyelashes.

It was the festive season; it was never too early for a Christmas drink.

NINE

KAMDEN

Gage won me the teddy; he scored enough shots on the Skee-ball machine, and I got to pick the teddy I wanted. I was so excited; I got the big bear with the blue eyes and brown fur.

"It's your reward for being good today," he said, kissing me on the tip of my cold nose.

"You think we can escape for a bit so I can give you a reward," I whispered, hugging the bear tight in my arms.

We took the bear up to the apartment and before Gage could say anything else, I was on my knees, ready to give him thanks. I pressed his back up against the window. If anyone looked up, they'd catch his bare cheeks squeezed against the windows.

I sucked his cock as if I hadn't eaten all day, this was my meal, and I was getting fed. His hands on the back of my head, back and forth, guiding me until he forced me to my legs.

"That's it," he said. "Your turn." He pushed the teddy against the window, then pushed me against the teddy. "You trust me, right?"

"Yes, Daddy," I giggled, wrapping my arms around the teddy.

Gage took control of my body; he removed my clothes with ease. A rustle of paper caused me to turn my head. He had the lollipops out. My hunger, a mixture of horniness and an actual empty stomach were strong.

"Open up and suck," he said, placing the strawberry lollipop on my tongue.

His warm, naked body hugged against mine. His kisses dripped down my neck, shoulders, and back, all the way to my ass.

It had been a short time of us together, but I'd gotten used to the way his body could control me, and the way it would move me in all directions. He parted my legs and arched my back in so my ass would present itself like the gift I was giving him.

He took the lollipop back from me and pressed it against my hole, he proceeded to eat my ass and play with the lollipop. Like he had done with the candy cane, he fucked me with it, and then ate the sticky sugary residue from my hole. My cock was completely solid, pressed against the soft fur of the teddy. I controlled the tingles as they spread throughout my body, curling my toes and squeezing my fingernails into fists to keep myself from exploring the deep pit of pleasure he woke within me.

"Your mine," Gage said, panting, out of breath as his lips touched my ear lobe. "And I don't want to let you go."

"Then fuck me," I said, gulping hard, once more, trying not to cum on the teddy bear. I didn't want to get it all wet and ruined, it was my new toy. "Please, Daddy."

His hard cock, resting between my cheeks, teasing my hole. It didn't take him long to slide a condom on his cock and then inside me. With the view of everything happening in the town square as the evening took hold and all the bright lights came on. My senses were being pleasured from both ends.

Fireworks went off, the first few bangs, Gage met them with thrusting rhythm.

The windows completely steamed over.

He pulled me in his arms, taking me away from the bear. He turned me around, switching things up as he lifted me into his arms and pinned me against the wall, his cock finding my hole after a few unsuccessful thrusts. Each thrust he nailed me harder against the wall, and I couldn't complain. It was hitting all the right spots.

The internal fireworks came. I grabbed my cock, forcing

it up against his abdomen from my position and shot my load up his chest. "Oopsie."

"I didn't say you could cum," he said, picking up the pace of his thrusts.

He didn't cum straight away after that, he kept going while I kissed his neck and played with his nipples at his request. My mouth working up to his ears, seeing if he enjoyed lobe nibbles as much as I did.

We moved to the bedroom, him carrying me on his hips. His cock came out of me a couple of times, then went straight back inside.

"I don't want to cum," he whispered, moaning at me. "I don't want to stop being inside you."

He laid me on my back in the bed, pushing my knees to my chest.

"You can stay inside me forever," I said, reaching up to his chest and with both hands I worked his nipples.

"Is that a promise?" he asked.

I nodded. I really did want him inside me forever. It would've meant he never had to go back home, and he would stay with me.

His cock pulsed inside me, filling the condom with cum.

For several moments after that, we laid together, his cock growing flaccid inside me.

My belly rumbled against his, breaking the cute moment. I giggled.

"We should go get something to eat," he whispered,

kissing me on the nose then my lips. He was slow to pull out.

Although I'd worked up a hunger, I didn't want to move from this position, and I didn't want to have to get dressed again.

He gave my thigh a gentle tap. "Come on," he said. "I also have to say bye to my folks, they're taking grandma with them to Connecticut tomorrow and I don't think we'll be awake early enough to see them before then."

Pressing my lips together, I was becoming emotional. He was involving me in his family.

I never anticipated what Gage and I had would've amounted to this, but it also was no surprise we were practically a couple at this point. I knew couples who moved faster after a single date. Sometimes when the chemistry is right and there, it's only natural for an explosion of fluids to happen, creating a bond between two people. We had a bond.

Gage continued to stay with me until his apartment was ready, and that was on Christmas Eve. We'd been in sync with each other, he took photographs of me, and I finished my painting of him. Neither one of us would let the other see what we'd been working on.

He woke me, not on purpose, he got a call from his friend, Alexia, telling him he could go back to the apartment. I knew it was coming, he'd already told me that Christmas Eve was the day after the fumigation.

"So, you're just going to leave me?" I asked once he finished with his call.

Standing in the doorway, trying to be quiet, Gage stared at me, shaking his head. "No, why would you think that?"

I turned over in bed and grabbed the enormous teddy. One of my Christmas wishes had come true.

"Don't start being a little sassy now," he snickered, climbing into bed and cuddling up to me. "I'm not going anywhere, yet. And I want you to come with me, I want you to meet my friend."

Backing up against his body, I didn't want him to leave the bed, or my body. But I knew the day would come. I often found myself getting bored of people easily, but with Gage, there was always something different, there was always something to keep me interested and occupied.

"Well, since you're leaving me today," I said, sighing. "I suppose I should give you your Christmas present."

"I'm not leaving you," he chuckled, rubbing his facial hair against my neck. "If anything, I'm inviting you into my life more. But if you give me my Christmas present, then I'll have to go downstairs to my car to get yours."

Immediately excited, I loved presents. "Is it big?" I asked, shuffling around in the bed to face him. "How big?" I held my hands out, giving a length.

"Bigger," he snickered. "Bigger than that."

"Will it hurt?" I whispered.

He wrapped his arms around me in a deep embrace and

kissed my forehead. "I hope not."

We both got dressed, the anticipation of knowing I was about to be given a gift had gotten me all types of excited. Gage commented about how after today he'll be able to show me that he has more clothes. It was a playful back and forth since I'd bought him those extra pieces of clothing to wear. And he refused to wear any of my underwear since most of them were a size too small and incredibly snug against my junk. It's how I liked it.

I hadn't wrapped my gift for Gage, I assumed I'd present it to him like a magician with an enthusiastic *ta-da!*

His gift was inside a large box. He'd wrapped it in red paper.

"Go on," he said. "Open it up."

That was all the permission I needed, I tore the paper to get to the box beneath it, and from there, I ripped apart the cardboard to find packing peanuts exploding out at me. Pausing, my head cocked to look at him. "What is it?"

"Be careful," he said, "empty some of them out and you'll see it."

Turning the box on its side to empty the squishy packing peanuts out, I saw the edge of a canvas. Immediately, I glanced at my stack of canvases against the wall and back to the edge.

"Well," he said, "take it out."

It was a photograph, stretched over canvas. Black and white. It was a photograph of me laid in bed, one of my ass cheeks out on show and my head buried into the pillow.

"Do you like it?" he asked.

I jumped into his body, swinging my arms around his neck. "I love it!" I smothered his face in kisses.

"You can see the little peach fuzz on your bum too," he said, pointing at the canvas.

"Ok, ok, you know I can't shave my bum."

He squeezed me. "I wasn't saying it's a bad thing. I love it."

"I didn't get to wrap your present," I told him. "So, close your eyes."

Gage placed his hands in front of his face, I trusted him not to peek.

The painting of him was dry, and I was nervous to show him. This was the first time I was showing someone my art in a while.

"Open." I held it in front of my face. I didn't want to see his reaction.

"Babe, this is—"

"Yeah?"

"Incredible."

I was marshmallow squishy, ready to melt into the floor. "You mean it?" I asked, lowering the canvas from my face.

"I mean it, I'd never lie to you," he said. "I—I love you."

"Oh. I love me too," I giggled. "You give me all the butterflies of love."

"You don't have to say it," he told me, cupping a hand

under my chin.

"But I do," I said. "I just think that if I say it, things might change."

"Then wait until you are sure things won't change," he said, leaning in to kiss me. "And you know, me having my apartment back won't change much. The only thing I hope that changes is you coming to mine and staying the night there."

I was looking forward to that as well. "I'm ready."

"Ok, so, are you going to hang my canvas of you, or are you going to hang your canvas of me?" His eyes turned to squinting question. "I mean, I'd love to hang this of myself, but I'd rather look at the one of you."

He was right. As much as I loved myself and my body, if he had the picture of me on his wall, he'd always be thinking of me. "Obviously, you should hang the one of me, maybe in your bedroom or something, I'll have to see what your wall space looks like first before we make any commitment on placing."

Gage didn't want to wait around to show me his apartment. I was nervous because I was being introduced to his friend who he lived with. Gage already knew my friend, Sian, who curated the local town gallery. And it was probably for the best that they knew each other, otherwise I might've been pushing for her to exhibit his photography.

He lived just outside of town in an apartment complex. They were busy with people driving in an out of the large parking lot. It was several floors of apartments, and Gage lived on one of the top floors. There was an elevator, people were lining up to get in it. Since everyone was coming back today, it was hectic.

We walked up several flights of stairs. I was sweating. It was made worse from all the layers of winter clothing, and also because the last time I went to a gym was in the summer.

At the door, a woman with a wild head of brown curly hair appeared.

"You must be Kam," she said, hugging me. "I'm sure Gage has told you all about me. Or not, you two probably had other things to do."

"Alexia," Gage said under his breath. "Don't scare him."

The apartment was nice, Gage showed me around, finishing the tour in his bedroom.

I laid on his bed and stared at the ceiling. The bed wasn't nearly as comfortable as my bed.

"Why do you look so sad?" he asked, snuggling beside me.

"After Christmas, we won't see each other as much."

"I told you we will," he said. "I'll still be working at the mall, and I need someone to kiss at midnight on New Year's Eve."

"I suppose my Christmas wishes came true," I whispered.

"What's that?" he asked. "You didn't tell Santa your

wishes."

I rolled over and laid on his chest. "You were my Christmas wish." It wasn't an exact wish for him, but he filled the hole of the wish, and every other hole in my body. The second wish was for a teddy large enough to fill the empty space in my bed. I got both.

TEN

GAGE

Kamden made it seem as if we would stop talking or even stop wanting to be in each other's presence once I was back in my apartment. It was the exact opposite. I wanted him to stay with me and he wanted me to stay with him. It was nice to have somewhere else to go when Alexia had her boyfriend over.

After Christmas, I was back at work and Kamden was sitting in the food court like a watchful little, waiting for me to have my break. He'd told me he was doing undercover security for his father, but I didn't believe that. There were rules to being in the mascot outfit, and one of them was that I wasn't allowed to speak, and I wasn't allowed to take it off where people could see me under it. Something about breaking the illusion, but we were a mall, not exactly Disney.

The window between Christmas and New Year's was both short and long. They were throwing the New Year's Eve party in the town center, and the previous year's I'd never been, I usually went into one of the bigger cities where I'd have tickets for an event. This year though, I had someone to kiss, and I didn't care about any event, all I cared about was kissing on the stroke of midnight.

In Kamden's apartment, both canvases were up on the bedroom wall. Kamden told me I needed to take the photograph to mine so that I would see his body every day. I saw his body every day anyway, I'd grown attached to it. He was almost a limb. I didn't know what I'd do if we had to spend the night away from each other. Kam would probably throw a hissy fit and I'd have to assert some Daddy dominance, but his sass would sometimes break me, and I'd end up giggling along with him.

"You know, we should've kept those outfits," he said, prodding me for attention as we both got ready for the grand countdown party. Standing in front of the full-length mirror together, he was half-naked from the waist down, and I was almost ready.

"Which ones?"

"Santa and the elf."

That was hot, I couldn't even deny. Santa always was someone you didn't want to fuck around with, and that was power. Kamden, while tall, and with facial hair, sure he wasn't the typical elf, but he was obedient where it mattered, and that's what counted. "You complained about yours being itchy," I said. "Maybe we can get our own set?"

"Really?" He grabbed my arm. "Because I'm totally down for that."

"Then we can do that," I told him.

He giggled with excitement, jumping onto his bed and grabbing hold of the teddy bear. "Yay!"

"Put some clothes on or I'll be forced to take a bite out of that juicy peach."

On his knees, arching his back, he wiggled his butt around. "It's Daddy's peach, you can bite it as much as you like."

I would've been tempted if I wasn't setting a good example. Alexia and her boyfriend were already at the bar across the street waiting for us. We were all going to meet up, drink, and then at midnight, we'd escape to the town center where the bell would strike midnight and the fireworks would go off. Although every time I kissed Kamden the fireworks were going off.

Dressing him in a pair of nice jeans and a shirt, Kamden admired himself in the mirror. "We're gonna have to dress this smart again when the gallery opens," he said.

"Smarter," I chuckled. "And we don't have to think about that yet, I'm still trying to narrow down the selection of photographs I want to put out."

He hugged me, squeezing me in at my side. "I still need my paint order to ship, otherwise I'll never get the perfect shade of—" I pressed a hand over his mouth.

"What?" I tried to get the information from him, but he was tight-lipped. He was very secretive about his art, and that made me all the more intrigued.

Snow fall was heavier, and everyone was out in the streets. Drunk people sang and threw snowballs at each other. Kamden, obviously wanted to try his hand at gathering up a snowball and immediately regretted it since snow was cold. I kissed his fingers as he pouted at me, trying to tell me about how the ice bit him.

It only got better, or worse, after that. The drinks came in. Champagne was popped.

The year had started off where I'd told myself I wanted to focus on putting my photography together for a portfolio. It also started how every year started, single.

Next year was going to be different. I was not going to be single, at least, I didn't think so. We had yet to define the relationship, and I didn't want to put that pressure on Kamden, although if I'd asked him to marry me, I'm sure he would've agreed. But we'd moved fast enough already.

Alexia prompted the question in the loud bar. "Dating? Boyfriends? You're not gonna pop the question at midnight, are you?"

"Boyfr—dating," I slurred.

"You want to be my boyfriend?" Kamden asked before

hiccupping.

"Do you want to be my boyfriend?" I countered.

Staring deep into his eyes, the sounds around us disappeared as we connected.

"Yeah," he said. "But on one condition."

Alexia huddled in as he spoke. "Oh, juicy, what is it?"

"Is this—" I tried to use telepathy, if there was ever a moment I had latent telepathy skills, it would come out now. I didn't have them. "What condition?"

"That we always sleep in the same bed," he said.

"Ok, my cue to leave," Alexia said.

I pulled Kamden into my arms. "I can agree to that," I whispered, kissing his cheek. "But my condition is that you have to give me a thousand kisses, every single day."

"A thousand?" he scoffed. "But I can't even count to that."

"You'll just have to try really hard then, won't you."

He puffed out his cheeks. "I'll try." He went in with kisses, smothering my face and neck in his ticklish pecks. "That has to be one hundred."

I overheard a comment shout that it wasn't even midnight yet.

It was always midnight with Kamden, kisses, fireworks, never wanting to leave the moment.

"I love you," he said.

"I love you too."

"Good, I thought you might've changed your mind," he

snickered. "Now, where did that bottle of champagne go?"

"Yes! Let's celebrate."

In my early twenties I was known for getting parties started, now, I was known for dipping out of them early. For him, I'd make the exception and stick around until we all went out for the big midnight countdown.

Announcing that I had a boyfriend wasn't as big of news as I wanted it to be. But that was probably the bubbles of champagne in my system. Although if my relationship with Kamden was going to compete with the celebrations of the new year, I could understand why they would fail.

I spotted couples, left and right as they all made out way before the countdown.

The baker and his boyfriend. Riggs and Tomas from the candy store. Alexia and her boyfriend.

If there was one thing I could count on feeling in December, it was a case of the hornies.

I grabbed Kamden by the hand and tugged on it for him to follow me outside. His face was all red and pink from the temperature inside the bar.

"Is it time?" he asked.

"I—I want to start the new year with a bang," I told him.

"You mean like—" He wiggled his brows at me.

"Yeah."

"Ok, Daddy," he pouted before biting his bottom lip. "How long do we have?"

Trying to focus my blurry eyes on my watch, we had over

fifteen minutes before the bell tolled midnight.

By the time we were back in the apartment, we had ten minutes. I didn't want to waste another moment not being inside him.

Kamden stood, giggling as I undressed him from head to toe. His cock was already hard. He tried to whack me with it as he swung his hips from side to side.

"I wanna watch the fireworks!" he said, pressing his naked body against the window overlooking the town square. His ass was a juicy peach, begging me to stuff it.

I sucked on my thumb to get it wet before hooking it inside him. He wiggled on it, then up and down as if it was my cock.

We had minutes until midnight and my cock was begging to be free so it could tear into Kamden's hole.

"Fuck me already," he said, his breath fogging up the window.

It took me right up to the one-minute mark to find the condom and lube, it would've been easier if I hadn't drunk so much.

He parted his cheeks for me to see his hole, teasing me as I lubed up my cock. Without warning, I thrust my body against his and my cock went deep inside.

"You like that?" I asked.

"Harder," he shouted. "I've been naughty."

"You have been naughty," I said, my mouth around his earlobe nibbling. "Teasing me with that perfectly round ass.

You don't like it when Daddy teases you."

"You—you—you always tease me," he moaned. His hands slapping against the fogged glass windows.

From the town square outside, the chorus of a countdown began. From ten, everyone was shouting. I timed the thrust of my hips to it.

At the stroke of midnight, the fireworks exploded in the sky, filling the darkness with color. The tolls from the bell were barely audible. My heartbeat was throbbing in my ears, thumping with the excitement of being inside Kamden.

Turning his head, we made out. Our bodies, connecting completely now.

We moved away from the window, almost kicking the small Christmas tree over on the coffee table as we moved.

On the sofa, against the wall, and finishing in the bedroom. Neither of us had cum. Both of our cock rock solid, waiting for the fireworks of an orgasm to explode.

We were worn out, laid together, side by side, my hand on his cock, his hand on mine.

He came first, the cum hitting his chest.

"Go faster," I instructed him as he slowed down, "and squeeze."

His jerked faster and harder than before. I rolled onto my side, my toes curling in anticipation. The fireworks popped inside. I came on his body. Slapping my dick in the cum on his stomach, he let out a giggle.

"It tickles," he said.

"I love you." I leaned in to kiss him.

"On a scale from zero to ten, how much?"

"Right now?" I asked, pecking at his neck with kisses. "A ten."

"And when is it a zero?" he grumbled.

"It's never a zero, sometimes it's a nine or an eight, but that's only when you don't listen to me," I admitted.

"You don't think we're moving too fast, do you?" his eyes grew serious for a moment.

It was something I'd been thinking about. "Time is weird."

"Doesn't answer my question," he sighed.

"It's weird because some things don't feel like they've happened as quickly," I said. "Me and you, it feels like it's been ages, it just feels like maybe that first night I stayed with you, it accelerated things. And I think it was a good thing, besides, we would've probably met at the gallery in February, I would've obviously fallen madly in love with you then."

Kamden gulped hard, like there was a lump in his throat. "You would've?"

"Of course. I think I fell for you when I first saw you," I told him. "The way you showed up in my life, it was like we both needed each other. We were being thrown together." I took his hand against mine, almost as if we were measuring fingers.

"I think we were."

"First, I was asked to be Santa, you were my elf, and then my apartment was fumigated, basically the world was throwing us together."

"And—and you're right, if we didn't meet then, we would've met at the gallery, and Sian would've told me about this handsome photographer. I'd have been jealous at first, because of your talent, obviously. Then—" He slipped his fingers between my fingers.

"And then what?"

"We would've fallen madly in love with each other," he snickered.

"You're my muse," I whispered, kissing his cheek.

"And you're mine." His voice cracked.

The universe really granted me my wish. I found someone I really liked.

EPILOGUE

KAMDEN

40 Days Later

My little stomach was buzzing with excitement and electricity. It had been so long since I'd shown anyone my art, and now it was going to be viewed by loads of people. The thought almost made me sick, but Gage was there, right by my side, holding my hand, whispering incoherently in my ear.

Gage was also showing his photography here too. It was the week before Valentine's Day, and the gallery had curated art from all mediums. The theme was the season of love. It was very on the nose considering. Gage's photography, while blurring my face was all about me, and mine was all about him.

Sian, my friend from art college stood at the doors of the gallery. She wore a pink striped suit and had her hair pulled back into a high ponytail. Immediately, I was snapping my fingers and telling her how gorgeous she was. I overcompensated with compliments when I was nervous.

"You two look adorable together," she said.

I would hope so. I was forced into a tight shirt and a pair of slacks. I felt like I was about to go into a school and teach a class.

"Just walk around, mingle, answer questions, you know," she continued.

We'd already taken the tour of the gallery yesterday. My pieces were beside his, nicely complimenting each other.

"Take a glass of champagne and if you're hungry, someone should be walking around with these mini pastries," she said. "Marcus, the guy who owns the bakery will make you wet, or as they say on that British baking show, give you a soggy bottom."

Gage chuckled. "You know, I think we'll save the soggy bottom for later."

Too stunned to speak. I grabbed a champagne flute.

Sian was entertained by the entire situation.

"It's going to be ok," Gage whispered, walking with our arms interlocked.

He was right. All I needed was to finish this glass of

champagne, and then take another glass.

My parents were both there supporting me, even if the idea of them seeing all the weird abstract paintings I'd done of Gage's naked body was throwing me. Or for them to see photographs of me, naked, but none of my actual goods on show. *Artist nudes*, Gage referred to them as, like an image you'd use on a dating app a hundred years ago.

There were also clay art pieces on display, it was about how different genitalia looked, and all of it had been painted to look like Chinese blue and white porcelain with the intricate designs, except, these had no function, only to be looked at.

Gage's family were here too. They were incredibly supportive, especially his grandma.

"Mom, you know you can't buy this piece," Gage's mom said. "You'll give someone a heart attack."

It was a black and white photo of me, with my face cropped out, but the booty was in view.

"I just want to pinch it," she said, reaching out with her hands like claws to the image.

Gage gave my butt a pinch. "Only I can do that," he said. "How are you enjoying?"

"Well, David is occupied over there," his mom said. "I think he's still trying to figure out what those things are over there." She gestured to the ceramics. "I don't have the heart to tell him, so I'm hoping someone else will."

My parents were in the section across from where my

paintings were.

The art wasn't realism, it was abstract, so there weren't any actual dicks on display, but plenty of phallic lines.

"We're spoiled for choice," my mom said. "We're thinking of getting one for above the mantel. You know, where the mirror used to be in the living room."

"I think we want this one," my dad said, sipping his champagne.

"This is the one I had to wait ages for the paint color," I said. "It's the exact shade of orange Gage likes."

"It is?" he said.

"Yeah, I thought you'd figure it out."

He smiled at me. "I figured you were mixing colors, but I didn't know you got this one specifically for me."

"I did."

He kissed me. People around us vanished from my mind, but they always did whenever our bodies connected. "I think I might need to take this one back myself."

"Not if I beat you to it," my mom said, pulling my attention away.

Gage pulled me close, holding me close at his side. "A bidding war?"

My mom scoffed, playfully. "So, you're trying to drive the price up."

"Is it working?" I asked.

"No," my father said. "For all the support we give you, we should be able to just take one."

We came to a compromise. My parents would not be taking any of the art and I would instead paint them something for their wall.

Together, we were a creative powerhouse. The two of us together, as we talked about our art to people. What he's said to me during the new year stuck with me, we really were destined to meet one way or another. And maybe before we even met, there were opportunities for the two of us to meet. I was in and out of the mall all the time, and that mascot was always there as well.

I think the moment I knew I really loved him was when we held each other's hands, and I wasn't nervous. I was comfortable; my palms weren't sweating. He stayed with me, protecting me, and becoming my muse to create from my heart.

I loved him so much, it hurt in the best way.

THE END

Make sure to check to come back and visit Hinton, New Hampshire in the *My Little's Wishlist* series.

AUTHOR'S NOTE

Hello reader,

I hope you enjoyed meeting Kamden and Gage, and I hope you'll continue the journey through Hinton as we get cozy with Riggs and Tomas at the candy store.

A huge **THANK YOU** to my 'Book Baby' supporters on Patreon who get exclusive and behind-the-scenes content, as well as advanced reader copies.

Tonya Polk, Bruno Neves, Cassie Geiger, David-Eric Nikielski, Fancy Tiefenau, JustToni, Willow Thomas, Tina Marie, Janet Hunt.

A special thank you to Cathy Christmas for her invaluable feedback.

And thank you for reading!

About the Author

JOE SATORIA is an MM romance author currently living in—who knows—anywhere in the world, really. He's a hopeful romantic—the hope being in his ability to one day find romance outside of fiction. And he's also a cat person—but deathly allergic to them.

If you can find me, follow me—I won't get a restraining order (this time).

If you love a good contemporary gay romance novel, I'll be serving it up to you from my favorite place in the world—my bed.

www.JoeSatoria.com

Made in the USA
Columbia, SC
19 June 2025